DISNEY PRINCESS

LOTS & LOTS OF
Look and Find®

pi kids®

An imprint of Phoenix International Publications, Inc.
Chicago • London • New York • Hamburg • Mexico City • Sydney

Welcome, everyone!

Are you ready
to have some fun?

Let's get started!

Look and Find

Look at the items in the colored border. Can you find them in the big picture? When you're finished, check the bottom corner for another challenge!

Look and Find

Briar Rose's fairy friends try their best, but their cake baking isn't always a great success.

These not-so-tasty-looking treats are for Briar Rose's birthday party. Can you spot them all?

won't-scream-for-ice-cream sundae

bleu cheesecake

apple turnover

pity-fours

sunken soufflé

To celebrate Briar Rose's birthday, can you help find 16 each of these things?

flowers   hearts   birds
candles   bows

38   39

What's Different?

When you see a pair of pictures, try to find what's different. There are 5 differences between each pair. Can you spot them all?

Ariel will need some magic if she's ever going to dance.

Search for 5 differences in Ariel's secret hideaway.

116   answers on page 122   117

3

Look and Find

When the prince asks Cinderella to marry him, it's the glittering start of her "happily ever after"!

Can you find these royal rings in the palace garden?

Jaq sees love is all around Cinderella! Can you spot these lovebird pairs here in the garden?

Look and Find

The entire kingdom is coming to Cinderella's wedding, and that means one very big dinner!

Can you spot these delicious dishes for the wedding guests?

Gus has found the food—he always does! Now, can you find these serving pieces to dish it up?

Look and Find

It's almost time for the wedding to begin…and Cinderella is just about ready.

Can you find these last-minute items Cinderella might want before she walks down the aisle?

Cinderella's Fairy Godmother hid these wedding gifts in her room. Can you find them all?

Look and Find

Flowers are everywhere as Cinderella and her prince walk down the aisle!

Can you find all of these beautiful bouquets?

Everyone is dressed up for the wedding. The Grand Duke is wearing his best monocle! Can you spot these fancy hats?

What's Different?

Cinderella loves her animal friends, and they love her too!

Can you find 5 differences
between the two pictures?

answers on page 20

What's Different?

With her friends' help, Cinderella has a pretty dress for the ball.

Search the sewing room
for 5 differences.

answers on page 20

15

What's Different?

Once it was a pumpkin. Now, with a *bibbidi-bobbidi-boo*, it's Cinderella's coach!

You won't need a magic spell
to find 5 differences here.

answers on page 21

17

What's Different?

Cinderella is a princess now—and the happiest girl in the kingdom!

Before the newlyweds run out of sight, find 5 differences in these scenes.

answers on page 21

What's Different?

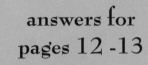

answers for
pages 12 -13

answers for
pages 14 -15

answers for
pages 16 -17

answers for
pages 18 -19

21

Look and Find

A princess can always use a little help from a four-legged friend, like Jasmine's racehorse, Midnight.

Whoa there! This marketplace is a bit of a mess. Can you spot this muddled merchandise?

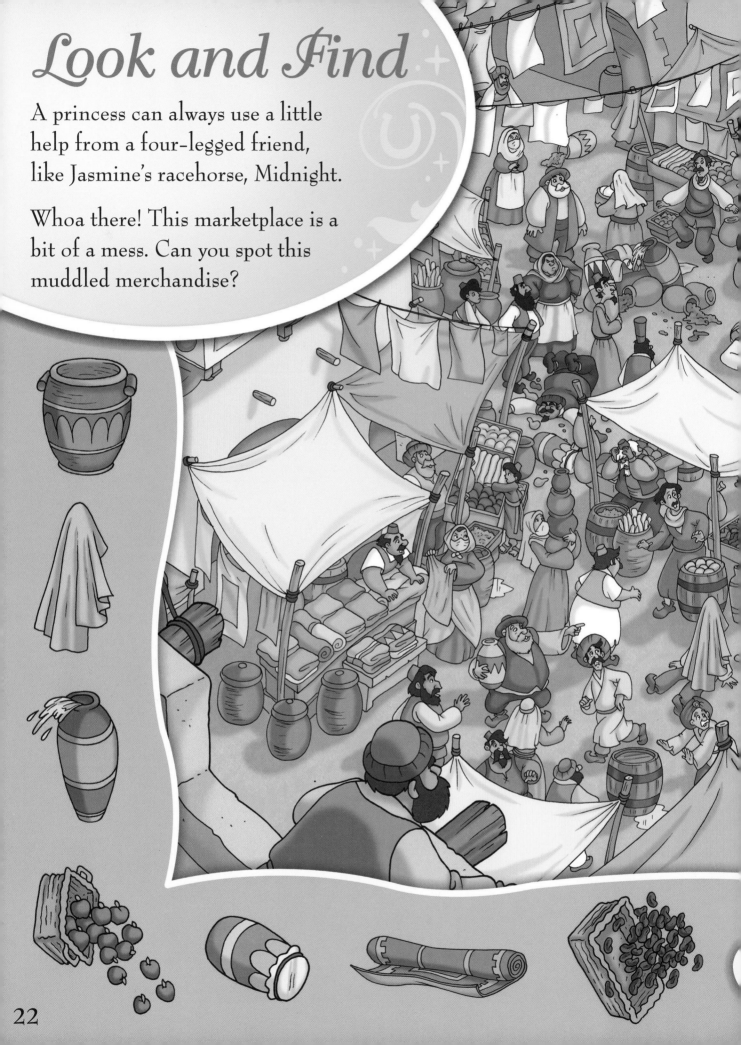

Aladdin wins by a nose! Now, can you find these surprised sellers and shoppers?

23

Look and Find

Mulan and her horse, Khan, are attending a grand Chinese New Year celebration. The village is full of people enjoying the festivities.

Can you spot these familiar faces in the happy crowd?

In China, every year is represented by an animal…including the horse! Can you find these other celebrated animals along the parade route?

dragon   sheep   dog   rooster

snake   tiger   ox   pig   25

and Find

...ing in the Mardi Gras parade. She's all dressed up for the party — and so is everyone else!

Can you find these costumed horses in the crowd?

Naveen has noticed that some costumes are very popular at Mardi Gras! Can you find these folks wearing the same outfits as the horses?

What's Different?

Mulan is a brave hero, on horseback and off.

Look for 5 differences
between these two pictures.

answers on page 36

What's Different?

Will Aladdin's new ride impress Princess Jasmine? It might...or might not!

Join the parade and find
5 differences between these pictures.

answers on page 36

What's Different?

Cinderella and Major are having a picnic with their friends. Yum!

Search this delicious scene
for 5 differences.

answers on page 37

What's Different?

It's the start of a new adventure for Merida and her horse Angus— straight out of a storybook!

Peruse these pages to find
5 differences between the pictures.

answers on page 37

What's Different?

answers for
pages 28 - 29

answers for
pages 30 - 31

answers for
pages 32 - 33

answers for
pages 34 - 35

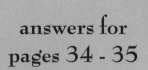

Look and Find

Briar Rose's fairy friends try their best, but their cake baking isn't always a great success.

These not-so-tasty-looking treats are for Briar Rose's birthday party. Can you spot them all?

won't-scream-for-ice-cream sundae

bleu cheesecake

apple turnover

pity-fours

sunken soufflé

To celebrate Briar Rose's birthday, can you help find 16 each of these things?

flowers   hearts   birds

candles   bows

Look and Find

Oh my! The fairies changed Aurora's pony Buttercup to match her favorite dress...but pink just isn't Buttercup's color!

Do you see these other pink things?

Fauna likes lots of different colors.
Can you find these colorful animals?

Look and Find

Briar Rose waltzed with her prince once upon a dream. Now that she is Princess Aurora again, her dream has come true!

Can you find these pairs of friends dancing at the ball?

42

Doesn't Aurora look lovely? Flora just wishes her dress was pink, not blue! Can you find ball gowns in these pretty colors?

red   yellow   orange

purple   green   brown

43

Look and Find

In a sparkling white wonderland of snow, it can be hard to find your woodland friends.

Search the scene for these snowy sidekicks:

Aurora counts on her
fairy friends to help make her dreams come true.
Can you count these things in the wintry glade?

3 snowmen   7 icicles

6 sleigh bells   8 red birds

When little Prince Phillip visits baby Aurora, he can't see what the future will bring.

Can you see 5 differences
between these two pictures?

answers on page 54

What's Different?

Briar Rose wonders if anyone will ever sing a love song to her. Soon, someone will!

Do you wonder if you can find 5 differences between these scenes? You can!

answers on page 54

What's Different?

50

Can you spot 5 surprising differences between these pictures?

answers on page 55

51

What's Different?

It's true love…at first sight.

Catch sight of all 5 differences in these two scenes.

answers on page 55

What's Different?

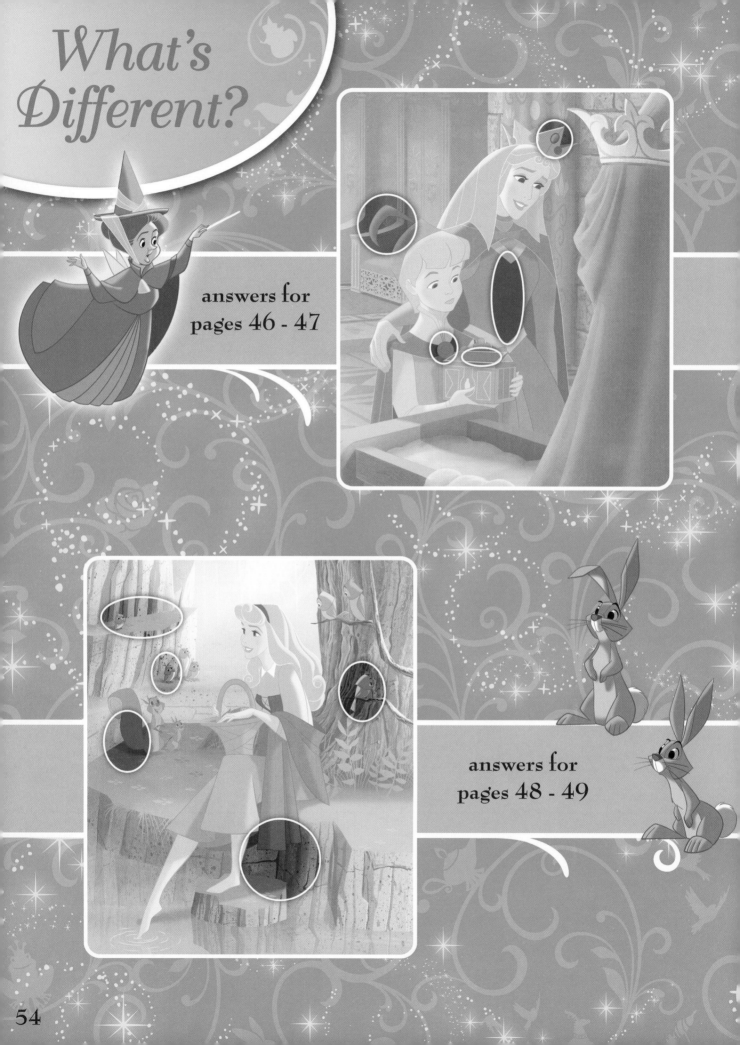

answers for
pages 46 - 47

answers for
pages 48 - 49

answers for
pages 50 - 51

answers for
pages 52 - 53

Look and Find

It isn't always easy to be a princess! Agrabah's royal rules say that Jasmine has to marry a prince before her next birthday…but none of these are her type.

Can you find all of Jasmine's unsuitable suitors?

Prince
Goodscents

Prince
Jewel Likeme

Prince
Abracadabra

Prince
Lotsachocolate

Prince
Jim Nastic

Prince
Nick Nack

Jasmine thinks that the princes' horses are much more interesting than their owners! Can you find these horsey things?

horse thief   horse fly

horse scents   Trojan horse

57

Look and Find

Snow White found a place to hide from the evil Queen, but it belongs to seven very untidy Dwarfs. It's time to clean up!

Help Snow White straighten up by finding these out-of-place belongings:

Bashful's
toy hedgehog

Grumpy's
rocks

ROCKS

Doc's inkwell

Sneezy's
flowers

Sleepy's
blanket

Dopey's alarm clock

Happy's
treasure chest

Most of the animals
are helping Snow White, but a few have found
other things to do. Can you find these creatures?

1 juggling bunny   2 soap-sliding bunnies

1 tightrope walker   3 rope-jumping squirrels

Look and Find

Today Mulan is meeting the matchmaker. She wants to make a good impression, but she'd rather train with a sword than wear a fancy dress.

Look for these things Mulan lost on the way to the matchmaker's:

jade necklace

parasol

cricket in cage

this fan

this apple

hair comb

60

The matchmaker's courtyard is a busy place!
Can you find these members of the crowd?

a well-groomed dog a woman with a powder puff

an elegant duck a man with a flowery fan

61

What's Different?

Gaston thinks he's the perfect match for Belle. Belle does not agree.

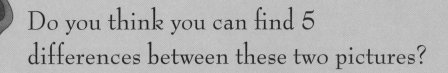

Do you think you can find 5 differences between these two pictures?

answers on page 70

What's Different?

Hmmm. Which Dwarf left this in the stewpot?

These pictures have 5 puzzling differences. Can you find them?

answers on page 70

What's Different?

66

Spot the 5 surprising
differences between the two pictures.

answers on page 71

What's Different?

Whoops! Mulan may need a little more practice.

Swing around and find 5 differences
in these two scenes.

answers on page 71

What's Different?

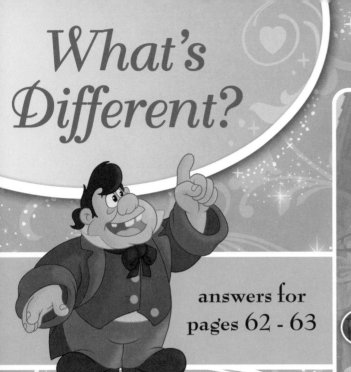

answers for
pages 62 - 63

answers for
pages 64 - 65

70

answers for
pages 66 - 67

answers for
pages 68 - 69

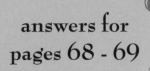

Look and Find

It was a happy day when Snow White met the Dwarfs—and vice versa!

Can you find these things that make Snow White smile?

fragrant
flowers

clean
dishes

pot of stew

basket of bows

baby bird

blueberry pie

These things make the Dwarfs smile.
See if you can spot them all.

Look and Find

The Seven Dwarfs are celebrating Snow White's happily ever after—with sets of seven surprises for her and the prince.

Can you spot them all?

seven gifts

seven letters

seven bouquets

seven photographs

seven cakes

Snow White will miss the Dwarfs when she moves to the palace. Can you find the gifts she's given them to remember her by?

Look and Find

What a lovely day for a picnic! There's something here for everyone, even the royal horses.

Do you see these treats a horse would enjoy?

bag of bran

horse biscuit

bowl of oats

hay

corn

sugar cubes

carrots

Now that the horses are fed, can you find these
delicious treats for the rest of the guests to enjoy?

sandwich   salad   cookies   lemonade

sausage   grapes   cake   chicken

Look and Find

Slipping, sliding, spinning, gliding:
everyone enjoys ice skating
on a bright wintry day!

Can you spot these
skating sweeties?

ice-dancing
deer

whirly bird

bouncing
bunny

twirling
squirrel

rambunctious
raccoon

clowning
chipmunk

galloping goose

The Dwarfs have stashed some cold-weather gear in case things get a little chilly on the ice. Can you find it all?

mittens   stocking cap   scarf

cape   earmuffs   muff

79

What's Different?

Snow White makes
a wish at the well.

Do you wish you could find 5 differences between the pictures? You can!

answers on page 88

What's Different?

Chores can be fun when friends work together!

Can you find 5 friendly differences between these two pictures?

answers on page 88

What's Different?

Dance around and find 5
differences between the two pictures.

answers on page 89

What's Different?

There are 5 differences between these scenes. Do you see them?

answers on page 89

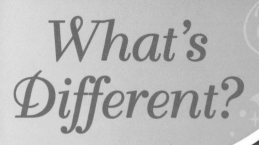

What's Different?

answers for
pages 80 - 81

answers for
pages 82 - 83

answers for
pages 84 - 85

answers for
pages 86 - 87

Look and Find

Belle's first visit to the Beast's library is a real eye-opener. She can't wait to start turning pages!

Open your eyes and find these books for Belle to read:

Beastly Ballads

True Fairy Tales

How to Break a Spell

Strange Science

101 Hair Bows

Why Petals Fall

Search the stacks for these things that will help Belle feel at home in the castle:

a picture of Belle's house

a picture of Belle's father

a horse figurine

flowers

Look and Find

It may be cold outside, but Belle is definitely warming up to the Beast! The Beast is making some feathered friends, too.

Can you spot these Beastly buddies?

red-head robin

love birds

bluebird of happiness

bald eagle   birds of a feather   hummingbird duet

Belle has read that
every snowflake is unique. Can you find these
one-of-a-kind specimens in this snowy scene?

93

Look and Find

Is the Beast falling in love with Belle? Everything he sees reminds him of his unexpected guest—including these ice sculptures.

Can you find them all?

books

mirror

Phillipe

rose

hearts

swan

Belle's new life in the
castle doesn't seem so cold with these friendly
servants around. Can you spot their icy images?

Cogsworth   Mrs. Potts   Babette

Lumière   Chip

Look and Find

Phillipe has a new roommate in the stables: a sweet little foal! People have been bringing her presents all day.

Try to find each of these welcoming gifts:

this basket of carrots

plush blanket

brush

these horseshoes

mane ribbons

grooming kit

The Beast knows that Belle has a soft heart!
Look around for 10 purple pillows she put in
the foal's new home.

What's Different?

Can you find 5 differences
between these two pictures?

answers on page 106

What's Different?

What's Different?

The Beast's servants welcome Belle with a fabulous feast.

Take a seat and look for
5 differences between the banquets.

answers on page 107

Belle loves her Papa too much to leave him forever.

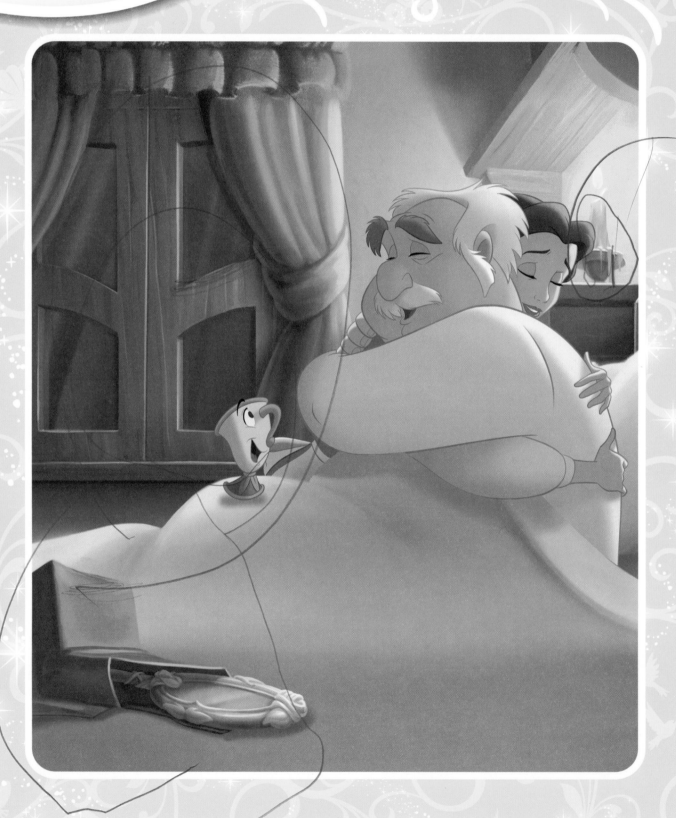

answers on page 107

What's Different?

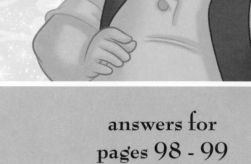

answers for
pages 98 - 99

answers for
pages 100 - 101

answers for
pages 102 - 103

answers for
pages 104 - 105

Look and Find

Merida wants a spell to change her mother...but the change might not be what she expects!

Look around for these magical gadgets:

the secret sauce

tongs

these dried herbs

welding mask

measuring spoon

mortar and pestle

Merida wonders how the witch can find *anything* in this cluttered cottage! Do you see these things in the muddle?

Look and Find

Pocahontas isn't sure John Smith understands how magical Nature can be. But she's determined to show him!

Can you spot these natural wonders?

eagle feather

seashell

this bird

this butterfly

blue jay feather

bear track

Pocahontas's world
is full of strange things—including unusual
animals! Which animals match these facts?

It sheds its skin as it grows.

It hunts from the sky at night.

It belongs to the same family as the dog.

111

Look and Find

Tiana and Naveen don't want to be frogs, but Mama Odie knows there's a difference between what you want and what you need.

Take a look around for these things Mama Odie needs:

Juju

bayou bugs

hot sauce

candy jar

magic potion

gourd

When Mama Odie
is not making magic, she's making gumbo!
Help her find what she needs for her next batch:

What's Different?

Love is the magical ingredient in Tiana's cooking.

Do you see 5 differences
between the two pictures?

answers on page 122

What's Different?

Ariel will need some magic if she's ever going to dance.

Search for 5 differences
in Ariel's secret hideaway.

answers on page 122

What's Different?

True love has broken
a beastly spell!

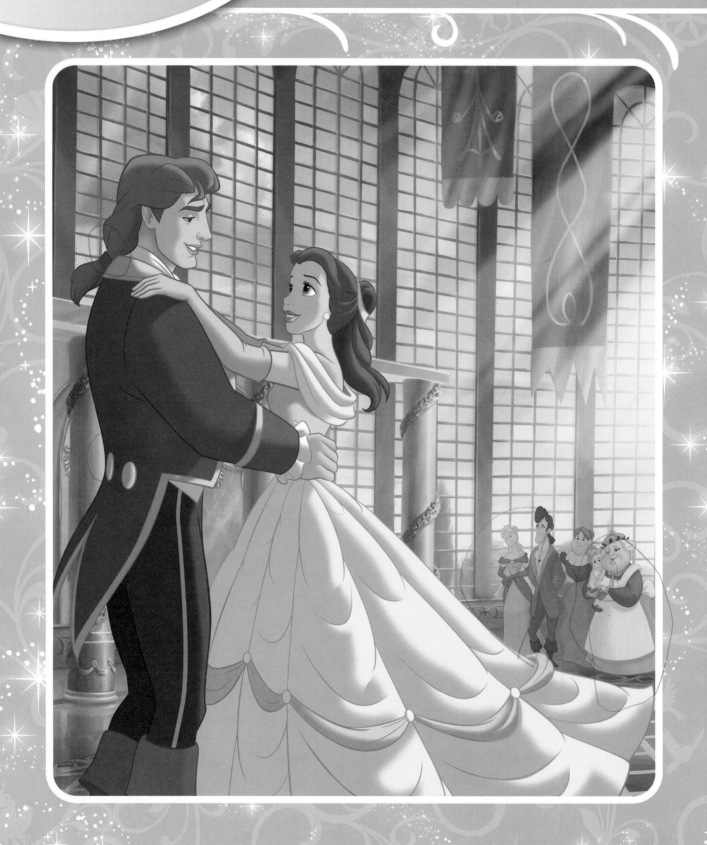

Find 5 differences between these two pictures.

answers on page 123

What's Different?

First meetings can be magical!

Look for 5 differences
around Pocahontas and John.

answers on page 123

What's Different?

answers for
pages 114 - 115

answers for
pages 116 - 117

answers for
pages 118 - 119

answers for
pages 120 - 121

123

Look and Find

Rapunzel doesn't know she is really a stolen princess. But she knows a lot about passing the time in her hidden tower!

Do you see some of Rapunzel's favorite ways to keep busy?

Rapunzel loves to paint! Look around the tower for these art supplies:

125

Look and Find

On her first adventure outside the tower, Rapunzel finds herself surrounded by ruffians with some surprising dreams.

Can you find these wishful wanna-bes?

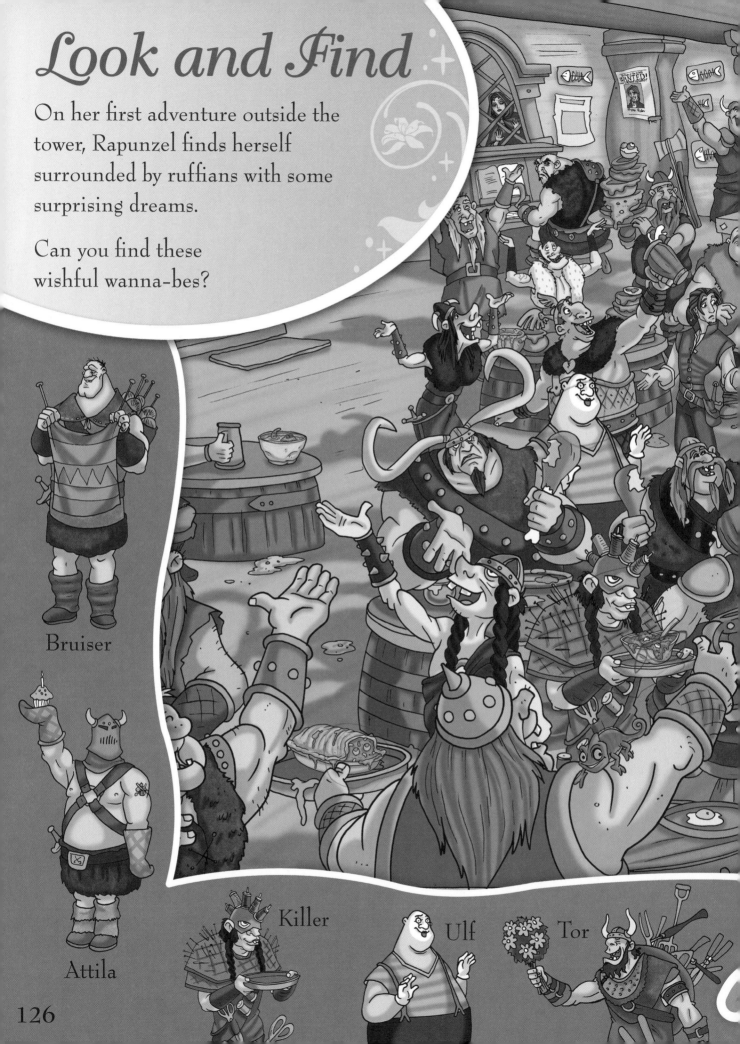

Bruiser

Attila

Killer

Ulf

Tor

Find yourself a bite to eat!

carcass casserole   petrified pudding   chocolate-covered crickets

127

Look and Find

Rapunzel has made it to the kingdom she's been dreaming about for years. But it's a dangerous place for her traveling companion, who is a wanted man.

Find these guards before they find Flynn!

Rapunzel sure likes lanterns!
Can you find 20 purple ones?

129

Look and Find

Rapunzel couldn't be happier! Now she knows she is a princess, and she has reunited with her parents.

Can you find these merrymakers ready to welcome her home?

No party is complete without gifts!
Can you find these?

golden
bowl

green sweater
with yellow stripes

pink frosted
cupcakes

131

What's Different?

Rapunzel shares a snack with Pascal.

Do you see 5 differences
between these tower pictures?

answers on page 140

What's Different?

Ready...set...go! Rapunzel and Flynn are off to the kingdom.

Search for 5 differences
between these speedy scenes.

What's Different?

Flynn's nose never looks right on the wanted posters!

Look right here for 5 differences between these city scenes.

answers on page 141

What's Different?

It's a night Rapunzel will never forget.

Don't forget to look for 5 differences
between the lantern scenes.

answers on page 141

What's Different?

answers for
pages 132 - 133

answers for
pages 134 - 135

140

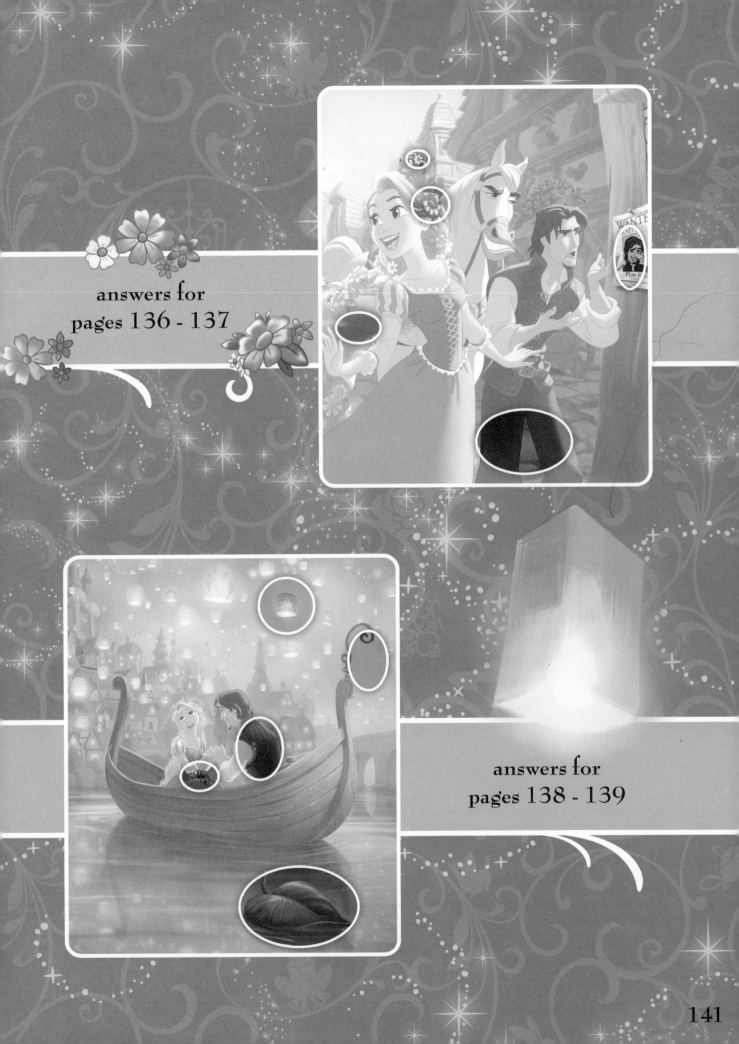

answers for
pages 136 - 137

answers for
pages 138 - 139

Look and Find

Merida is tired of her mother's lessons! She leaves the castle behind and finds freedom in the forest with her horse Angus.

Search for these falcons, whose mothers never tell them what to do!

Can you score a bull's-eye by finding these targets Merida made for herself?

143

Look and Find

Merida discovers that the demon bear Mor'du was once a prince whose wish for the strength of ten men went very, very wrong...just like Merida's wish for her mother.

Search Mor'du's lair for these mystical carvings:

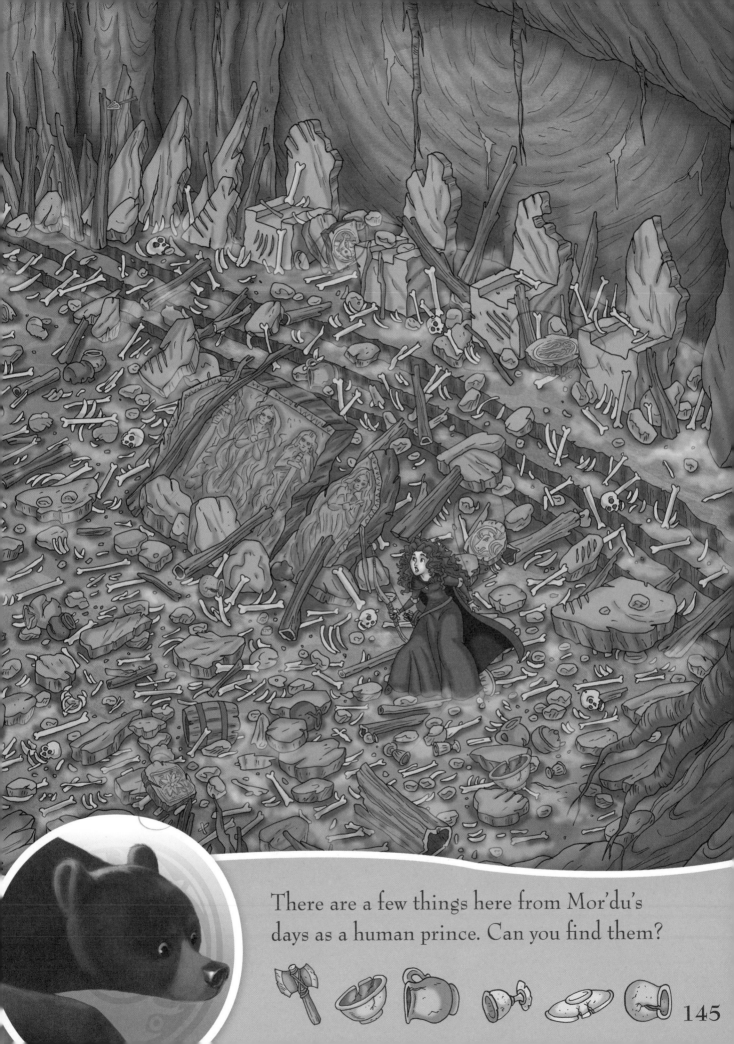

There are a few things here from Mor'du's days as a human prince. Can you find them?

Look and Find

Merida risks her life to save her mum-turned-bear from a hunting party. She really does love her mother!

Try to find these bear-hunters' weapons:

Will o' the wisps are a sign that magic is near.
Can you find and count two dozen at the hunt?

Look and Find

Merida and her mother are making a new tapestry that stitches the whole family together.

Look around to find these woven images from generations past:

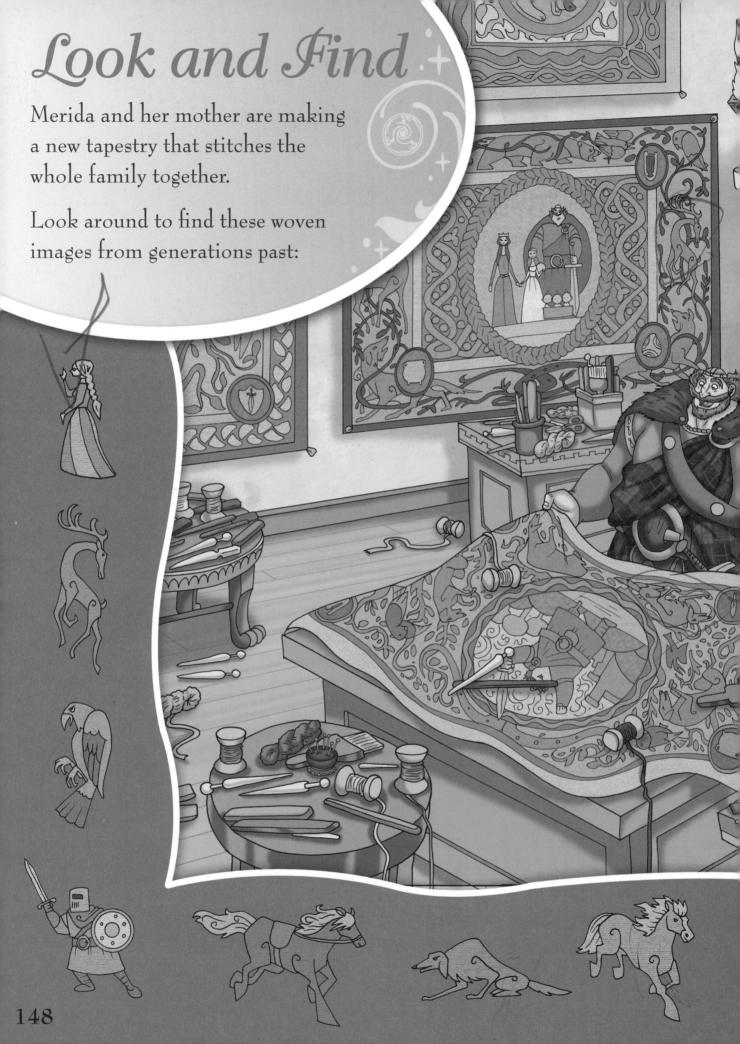

Queen Elinor thinks
that Merida can use a sewing lesson or two. Or six.
Look for these sewing supplies to get her started:

149

What's Different?

Queen Elinor is determined to turn Merida into a proper princess.

Can you spot 5 differences
between these pictures?

answers on page 158

What's Different?

Merida has three little brothers: Hubert, Hamish, and Harris.

Can you find all 5 differences between
one set of triplets and the other?

answers on page 158

What's Different?

Do you see 5 differences between these royal representations?

answers on page 159

What's Different?

Merida is brave, and her mother is proud of her!

Look for 5 differences
between these tapestry scenes.

answers on page 159

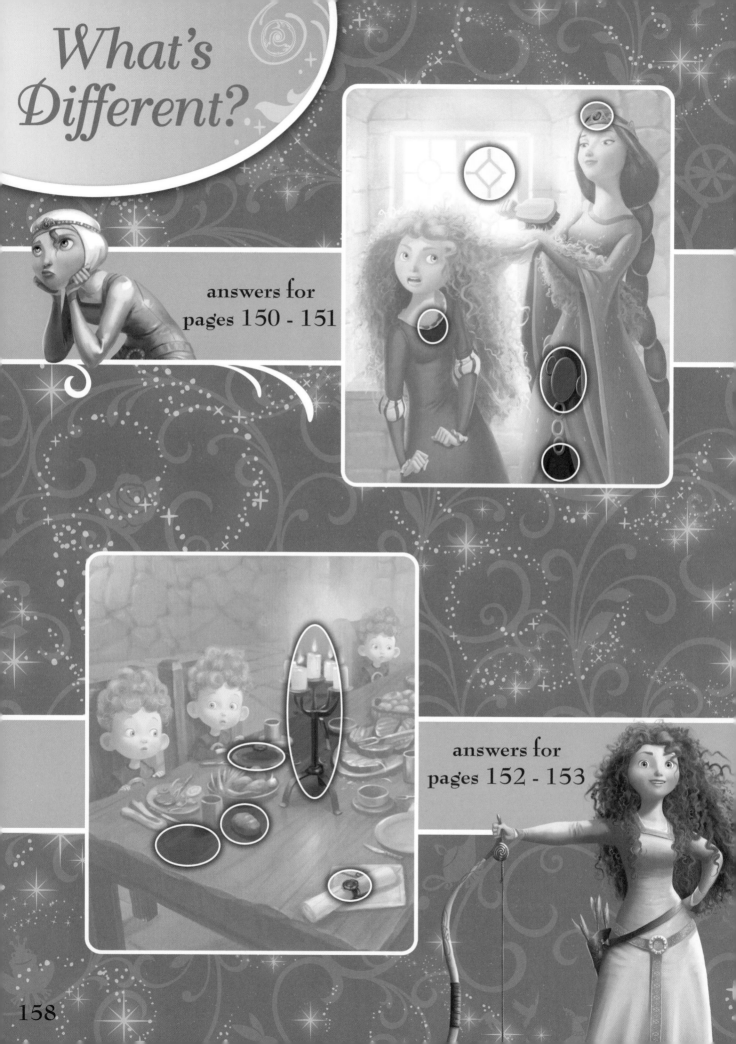

What's Different?

answers for
pages 150 - 151

answers for
pages 152 - 153

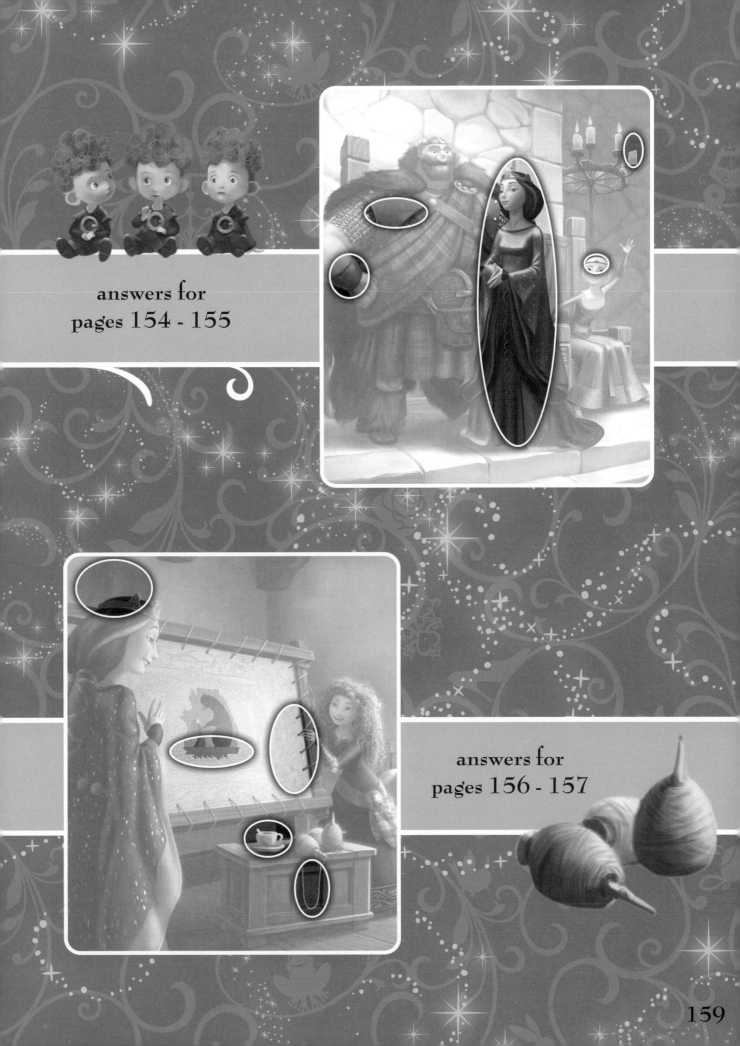

answers for
pages 154 - 155

answers for
pages 156 - 157

159

Look and Find

Dreams *do* come true. It took hard work and a little bit of magic, but Tiana's Palace is finally open for business!

Can you find all of today's menu specials?

The food is hot, and
the music is smoking! Can you spot these members
of Naveen's jazz band?

Look and Find

Jasmine dreamed about the world outside Agrabah's palace. Now she's seeing it from a flying carpet!

Can you pick out these colorful cottages?

Jasmine and Aladdin
aren't the only ones enjoying the view from above.
Can you find these feathered friends?

163

Look and Find

Rapunzel has wanted to visit the kingdom for as long as she can remember.

Can you spot these villagers doing things she always wished she could do?

celebrating

flying

riding

running

splashing

dancing

Rapunzel is living her dream. So are these friends of hers around the square. Can you find them?

What's Different?

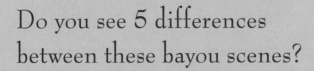

Do you see 5 differences
between these bayou scenes?

What's Different?

It's time to celebrate!
Aladdin is *Prince* Aladdin now.

Look for 5 differences between these rooftop representations.

answers on page 174

What's Different?

Rapunzel's first visit to the kingdom is a dream come true!

Look around for 5 differences
between the marketplace pictures.

answers on page 175

What's Different?

Ariel tells her dreams to her horse, Beau.

Trot around and find 5 differences between the stable yard pictures.

answers on page 175

What's Different?

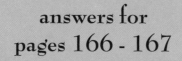
answers for
pages 166 - 167

answers for
pages 168 - 169

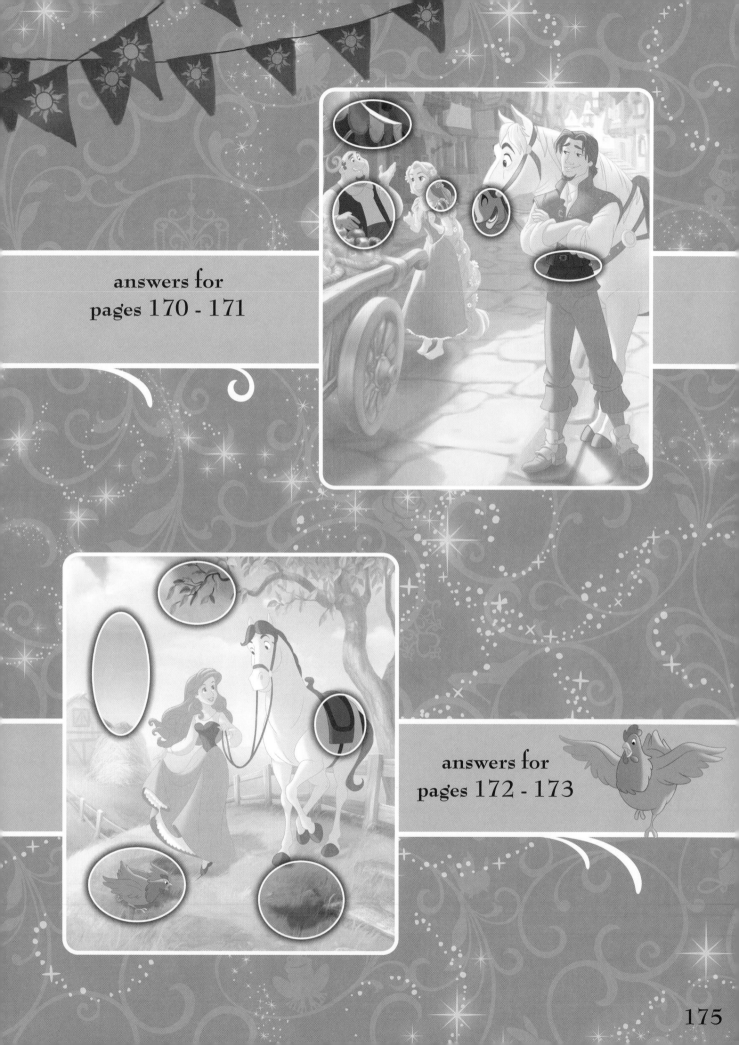

answers for
pages 170 - 171

answers for
pages 172 - 173

Look and Find

Ariel loves to explore sunken ships and collect treasures from the human world. But her fishy friends wonder what all the fuss is about!

Who is keeping Ariel company as she explores?

sapphire bluegill

goldfish

ruby-red snapper

silver swordfish

crowned cod

It takes a long time for an oyster to make a pearl. Take your time and find these pearly pieces in the ship:

pearl earrings   pearl bracelet   string of pearls

pearl ring   pearl brooch

Look and Find

Ariel spent the day dreaming about life on land…and forgot all about the royal concert! Will she make it to the stage on time?

Search the scene for Ariel's six singing sisters:

Aquata

Andrina

Arista

Alana

Adella

Attina

Sebastian wants everyone to put their claws together for Ariel's backup band. Can you find these musicians?

clambourine   guitarpon   lutefish   179

Look and Find

Ariel loves everything about life on land, and that includes horseback riding! She's throwing a party for her new horse, Beau.

Can you find the gifts Eric's loyal subjects have brought for the party's guest of honor?

saddle

horseshoes

this gift box

horse treats

grooming brush

blanket

Beau isn't the only animal at the party! Can you find these other animal friends around the beach?

1 dolphin   4 cats   13 seagulls

3 squirrels   5 dogs

Look and Find

Ariel is celebrating her first holiday season on land by surprising her friends and family with gifts.

Shop around and find these treasures for people on her list:

dog dish

pocket watch

shell ornament

nautical pendant

music box

ship in a bottle

Can you find a snow globe Ariel might like?
(Scuttle's favorite is the dinglehopper.)

183

What's Different?

Looks like everyone in Atlantica is on the way to Ariel's concert!

Can you find 5 differences
between these underwater scenes?

answers on page 192

What's Different?

The star of the show is missing!

Find 5 differences between these
two pictures. Then take a bow!

answers on page 192

What's Different?

Ariel likes human objects...but she doesn't always know how to use them.

Comb through these two scenes to find 5 differences.

answers on page 193

What's Different?

It's happily-ever-after time for Ariel and Eric.

Can you find all 5 differences
between one farewell scene and another?

answers on page 193

What's Different?

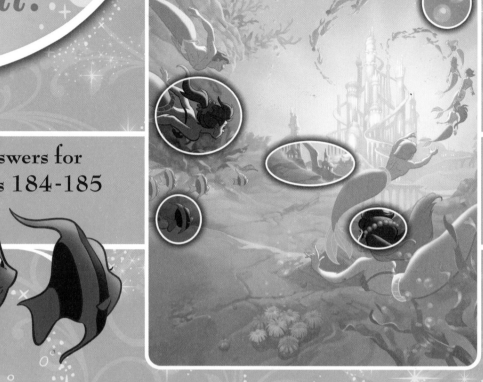

answers for
pages 184-185

answers for
pages 186-187